THE MILL

Mark West

Greyhart Press

Mark West

THE MILL

ISBN 978-1475085242

Also available as
Amazon Kindle book ASIN: B005QBY84M
ePUB eBook ISBN: 978-146581711

Published by Greyhart Press
www.greyhartpress.com

An earlier edition of this novelette was published in paperback by
Pendragon Press in 2008 as part of the collection We Fade to Grey
(ISBN 978-0955445286).

For
Alison & Matthew,
as always.

1.

The trees around him were bare and there was a strong chill in the air that raked his throat as he breathed. A crow cawed loudly, as if he was getting too close to its nest.

He was in a clearing that felt familiar though he couldn't place it. Ahead of him was a fence, splintered wooden posts set at six-foot intervals, draped with barbed wire and just beyond that a rough-looking hedge. Spindly trees were dotted around, the tips of their apparently hollow trunks knocking against one another in the breeze and sounding like damped bamboo wind chimes. To his left were more trees, thicker with dense foliage and a narrow path led between them into depths that seemed to pulse with darkness. To his right, a mound of earth rose sharply to the height of a double-decker bus and he climbed up it, so that he could get his bearings at the summit. The top of the mound was sunken, littered with the detritus of winter.

From this vantage point, he could see that he was surrounded by fields and a couple of stands of evergreen trees. Ahead, the sun was setting behind another copse, but this one was different, bigger, the branches of the trees spreading out as if they were sheltering something.

He saw movement at the copse and shielded his eyes, squinting into the dying light. There was someone there, a woman with long red hair, wearing a pale dress.

He had to reach her, to find out where he was and he started down the mound, slipping and sliding. At the base, he stumbled and felt a sharp pain in his ankle but ignored it, got to his feet and ran, as best he could, to the gap in the hedge.

"No, don't."

The voice seemed to come from all around him and he stopped, looking around. "Nic?"

"Don't go, Michael."

At that, as always, Michael Anderson started awake. Quickly, he looked at Nicola's side of the bed but, as usual, it was empty.

"Bugger," he said and closed his eyes.

2.

It was a cold evening in early October and the rain, which had been threatening all day, was now falling as a drizzle.

Michael Anderson pulled into the small car park at the end of Duke Street. Broken glass glittered in his headlight beams, like a carpet of diamonds.

There were four other cars parked, the occupants barely visible behind the misted windows but he didn't glance at them as he got out, locked the car and walked to the pavement where the lights from the Duke Street Community Centre splashed across the paving slabs. He couldn't see or hear anything but knew that Drew would be inside, bustling about and setting the room up, waiting for the bereft and lonely to turn up, to try and take comfort from others, sharing a camaraderie they desperately wanted but couldn't quite give.

Michael wasn't blessed with a photographic memory but now, sometimes, he wished he was. There was one thing he remembered vividly though, from the summer before last, which had been long and hot, the temperatures breaking all previous records.

They were on the patio. His wife, Nicola, was in the sun topping up her tan whilst he was sheltering under the umbrella. He watched a bead of sweat slide from her neck into her cleavage, which glistened with sun lotion.

"Isn't this great?" she asked, turning her head to look at him, shielding her eyes. "We're happy and healthy and it's a lovely day. Could life get any better?"

"No," he said and leaned over, to kiss her, "I don't think it could."

A narrow corridor led to the Community Centre's main hall, where the Tots & Toddlers group met. Small tables and chairs were stacked neatly along one wall, coat hooks above them as high as Michael's waist and the far wall was covered with impressionistic images that only the artist could identify. The floor, marked out for games of football, tennis or basketball, always looked clean but felt gritty to him, as if the kids had brought sand in from somewhere and it had shaken out of the grips of their shoes during the day. The room had a peculiar smell, at once sweet and sour and he now associated it — must and warm bodies and budget cleaning fluids — with the thought of death.

The Bereaved Partners' Group met in a small anteroom and through the open door Michael could see several people, their backs to him, making drinks. Drew was perched on the edge of a table, flicking through some papers and, as if he could feel Michael watching him, turned and smiled.

"Good evening," he said, "how are you?"

"Not brilliant," said Michael, as he went in and shook Drew's outstretched hand.

"Oh." Drew was somewhere in his early fifties, a short podgy man with thinning hair who dressed in very rich colours. Michael didn't know what had happened to Drew's partner, except that he'd been in a hospice for a long time and had died last year. "I know you don't want to hear this, but it does get easier. Never better, absolutely not, but it does get easier."

Michael felt his eyes warm with tears, as they often did at these meetings. He didn't want life to be easier to live without Nicola; that didn't seem at all right and listening to his fellow Group members, half of them felt the same way. Drew seemed to notice his discomfort and nodded, so Michael hung up his coat — the pegs set at an adult height in this room — then went over to the refreshment table to make himself a cup of tea.

"I don't know how much more I can take, I'm not sleeping, I feel awful, nothing seems important anymore."

As he grieved, Michael suffered with insomnia. Between Nicola's passing and the funeral, he'd survived on little more than cat naps but everyone told him that was natural and he felt so bad anyway, the tiredness didn't register with him.

Doctor Colbert looked at Michael through steepled fingers. "Michael, you have to accept you've suffered a massive trauma, a massive loss, at a

5

relatively early age. You need to deal with it yourself and, I'll be frank, I'm reluctant to prescribe you too much."

His condition slowly improved after the funeral, as he moved into a new routine. He'd potter around the house, eat, go out for long walks and veg out in front of the TV. As the clock rolled past midnight, he'd go to bed and lie in the darkness, willing sleep to come. It often took a while and he'd lay and watch the lights from cars outside dance across the ceiling or listen to people as they walked by. He'd hear human life, outside the four walls of his house, going about its business whilst inside, with him, there was only silence.

"I am dealing with it, every day when I open my eyes and the other side of the bed hasn't been slept in."

"Michael, I've been your doctor for a long time, Nicola's for even longer and what happened to her was just…" Colbert paused for a moment, as if trying to decide how best to express himself. "Well, it was very aggressive and you need time to deal with that, to process your thoughts and reactions." Colbert reached for his prescription tablet and began writing. "I can give you something to deal with the insomnia and some of the feelings, a course of Mirtazapine. It'll help but not necessarily for the long term, for that I think you'll need to speak to people."

"I don't want to go to a psychiatrist."

"I was thinking more of a local group, for people who've lost partners."

"A group?"

"Just give it a chance, okay? You'll meet people in the same position, who'll know how you're feeling and might have suggestions on how to deal with your emotions. You can talk, work through issues, realise that you're not alone. The guy who runs it lost his partner and he believes it was the group that helped to pull him through the worst of it all."

Michael stared at the wall behind the doctor, where three fingerpaint drawings were tacked below his medical certificates. Below them was a framed photograph of an attractive blonde woman holding a curly haired blonde toddler.

"Okay," he said finally, "if you think it'll help, I'll go."

Michael did find the group useful, though he rarely spoke in discussions and didn't feel that he'd particularly opened up. But that didn't matter, listening to others had been helpful. Part of it was the strength these people displayed — the matter of fact way they discussed how their spouses were taken from them, some suddenly but most having succumbed to an illness that, more often than not, left them a shadow of their former selves. Not all of the attendees spoke and some of them didn't seem particularly friendly but Michael could see that by the end of each evening, their spirits were raised — however slightly — as were his, until he drove home to the empty house.

Drew did a good job, keeping the group as informal and light as he could and now, he was shooing people to their seats, checking his watch theatrically.

"Come on folks, we don't have all night."

A couple of people laughed and joked with him, calling him a control freak. For some reason, the idea of that — and looking at Drew's pretend-outraged face — made Michael smile.

"Well that's nice," said a woman beside him.

Michael turned. "Hello, Saskia," he said. "What's nice?"

"You smiling." She looked at her hands, as if suddenly embarrassed. "It's nice to see you smile, I mean."

He nodded and sat next to her. "Thank you."

"You're welcome."

He'd spoken to Saskia a couple of times and they often sat next to one another. A tall, slim redhead, she was the only person in the group younger than he was. He didn't know the story behind her loss, since neither of them had asked the other, their conversation skirting the topic like an expert skater.

They looked at one another, not needing to ask silly questions about how the other felt. She offered him a lazy smile, as if in compensation.

"It's good to see you," he said.

"And you."

Drew finally got as close to his silence as he was likely to and sat on the edge of the desk. He ran through some news items, local events that might interest the group, but nobody took him up on any of them so he put his papers back into a folder.

"Tonight," he said, "I thought we'd discuss 'The Grief Cycle'. I know I've touched on this before, but we have some new members now," he gestured towards Michael and Saskia, "and it might be good for them to know about it."

Someone said "I found it very useful" and Michael nodded, wishing that he hadn't been singled out.

"This isn't a new concept," said Drew, "but I think it works and I like it. In essence, it states that there are sequential stages to grief, hence the idea of a cycle and, generally speaking, most of us will be affected by at least some of these stages."

Michael loved pretty much everything about Nicola and he loved looking at her. If she noticed him, she always told him to stop, said it made her self-conscious, but he couldn't help it.

Now, he could pinpoint the exact time that his world, as he loved and understood it, began to crumble around him.

It was a normal Wednesday morning and he'd just had a shower. Nicola was standing at her dresser, doing up her bra strap and he stood in the doorway, watching her. The early morning sun, diffused by the net curtains, gave her a glow, glints of light colouring her bare back and legs. Her hair was loosely pulled up, stray strands brushing the back of her neck.

"Mrs Anderson, you look beautiful."

Nicola turned to face him and fluttered her eyelids. "Flatterer."

"Will it get me anywhere?"

She smiled and raised her left eyebrow. "Often."

He laughed and walked up behind her and pulled her tight to him. She wiggled her behind against his groin and giggled. "You like that, eh?"

"Of course," he murmured, kissing her neck gently and slid his hands up her belly. Her bra wasn't clipped together and his hands ran under the cups, gently squeezing her breasts. He heard her sigh and then he felt it.

"What's that?"

"What?"

"There's something under your left boob."

"What? Where?" She pulled her breast up, feeling underneath with her fingers delicately. He guided her hand until she found the bump and looked at him. "What is it?"

He crouched down. "I don't know, sweetheart, I can't really see anything."

"It's probably nothing," Nicola said and smiled a fragile smile.

"The first stage is denial," said Drew. "When I lost Simon, it took me a long, long time to believe it and I was convinced, for ages, that he'd walk through the door at any moment, smiling his big, silly grin and asking me why I looked so sad."

Drew stopped for a moment, as if to gather himself. Someone across the table from Michael coughed, but otherwise there was silence before Drew carried on.

"Anger next, aimed at either the departed, or yourself, or whichever God you happen to believe in. Or at a third party, of course, if you'll forgive me mentioning it, Bridget."

Michael glanced over at Bridget, who was staring at the table, dabbing her eyes with a tissue. What was her story, what rage did she feel?

"Then there's bargaining, which — with hindsight — is frankly silly but I did it, I begged God many times to spare Simon and take me instead. That's when I hit rock bottom, I think and that led me straight to the next stage, of depression."

"Amen," said somebody quietly.

"We all know about this and all of us will have a different reaction. There can be tears or no tears, rage or no rage, any number of feelings, but it doesn't matter if what you feel isn't what the books tell you to feel. The way I reacted, I know, isn't what happened with others."

"That's right," said a man across from Michael. "I internalised everything and made myself very poorly for a long time."

"Thank you, Bill", said Drew. "From here, we move to the last stage, of acceptance, where we're ready to accept what's happened and move forward."

"Are you there, Drew?" asked Bill.

Michael watched as Drew swallowed, looked nervously around the room and touched his Adam's apple gently. "Some days I am," he said finally, "but other days I'm not."

3.

Michael was at work when Nicola called. She'd made an appointment but insisted on going alone and he sat at his desk, waiting for her call, trying to concentrate on his computer monitor but failing miserably. He knew it was probably nothing, perhaps even something as silly as heat-rash, but he also knew that Nicola's aunt had had a mastectomy three years ago.

"They don't know what it is," she said. "I'm being set up with an appointment at the hospital."

There were a lot more appointments and phone calls and then, three months shy of her thirty-third birthday, Nicola Anderson was diagnosed with ductal carcinoma.

Michael knew that the doctor, who didn't look old enough to have done all of his necessary training, wasn't trying to be brusque but it sounded like it — to him, it was business as usual, to the Andersons it was earth-shattering news.

"What kind?" asked Nicola.

"IDC," said the doctor, "it's quite a common type." He searched his cluttered desk for an X-Ray wallet, took out the negative and slapped it onto a lightboard.

"That's the culprit, the blob with the spines coming out of it."

"What happens now?" asked Nicola. Michael noticed that her arms were crossed over her chest.

"Well judging by the size, we've hopefully caught it early enough to treat it, though people obviously react differently."

"Could you be wrong about any of this?" Michael asked.

The doctor pursed his lips and shook his head. "It's highly unlikely, the biopsy just confirms what we can see with the X-Ray."

"So what happens now?" asked Nicola again, her voice sounding a million miles away.

"We treat it, Mrs Anderson, to try to get rid of it."

But, even though Nicola was treated promptly and thoroughly, they couldn't. Within a couple of months they were sitting in a consultant's office, which had a nice view of the grounds and plenty of spare desk space. Michael didn't think he'd ever felt so nervous in his life and the fact that Nicola was gripping his hand as if she was hanging off a cliff didn't help.

"Mrs Anderson," said the consultant, leaning forward, his hands pressed hard on the desk. "I'm afraid that I have bad news."

"Tell me," she said, her voice tight.

The consultant cleared his throat. "Have you ever heard the word metastasis?"

Michael had and felt his world give way, as a wave of nausea washed over him. Nicola had researched her condition on the Net and metastasis was just one of the fun new words they'd discovered.

"Yes," said Nicola. Michael squeezed her hand and swallowed back bile.

"I'm afraid, Mrs Anderson, that as we suspected, you have a very aggressive cancer and, unfortunately, the metastasis is widespread."

"Lung?" asked Nicola quietly.

The consultant nodded. "It's also showing in your bones and pancreas. I'm very sorry."

Michael looked at his wife, the tears gleaming on her cheeks and the consultant, who looked between them gravely. He couldn't take any of this in, didn't want to hear it, just wanted to be back in the bedroom, holding his wife tight.

The cancer attacked Nicola without mercy. Sometimes, Michael would go to work and, on his return home, be able to see a difference in her, even if in some indefinable way.

Too soon, she was admitted to hospital and then to the Church View hospice, where she would eventually see out her life. Michael grew to hate the place. It looked imposing as you drove towards it, with bright red bricks and brown windows and white fascia, but close-up it was like any other building where profit wins over compassion. The bricks were starting to crack, some of the double-glazing was fogged and the plastic fascia was peeling at the corners.

Nicola's room, which looked out onto the brick wall of a haulage company's yard, was small and functional, never entirely clean but not exactly dirty either. Michael called in on his way to work, spoke with the staff to find out how her night had been and then called in on his way home from work to sit by his wife's bed until they kicked him out. Then he'd pick up some food and go home, wishing his life could go back to how it was before, with Nicola by his side.

As her condition worsened, the mental toll on him worsened. Sometimes, he didn't think she was his wife, the gorgeous vivacious woman he'd married, who reached for his hand whenever they were out walking and giggled like a schoolgirl if he told her the most stupid of jokes. No, this poor wreck of a woman, who didn't move and slept a lot and smelled vaguely of antiseptic, was someone else — an impostor, imperfectly made because Nicola had never looked this frail. He couldn't hear her breathing as she slept, however close he sat and contented himself with the shush of the morphine slide, hidden under the bed covers. It wasn't the same, but it was something.

The night before she died, as he prepared to leave, he leaned down to kiss her. She moved her head slightly and their lips touched.

"Goodnight," she managed to whisper.

He smiled. "G'night, beautiful, I'll see you tomorrow." He kissed her again and went home.

Nicola passed away just after ten, on an overcast Wednesday morning. Michael stood next to her mum, who dabbed her eyes with a handkerchief. Her dad was on the other side of the bed, biting his lip and trying to remain stoical.

The attending nurse confirmed that she was gone, then opened the window. Nicola's mum burst into loud, wracking sobs, and Michael and Nicola's dad looked at one another, unsure of what to do.

He drove his in-laws home, sat in the lounge with them, made strong, sweet tea and poured a large slug of whiskey into his father-in-law's glass. He went through old photo-albums with them, which ran from the early seventies, with bright, almost Technicolor photographs of a toddler Nicola running around on the beach right up to the mid-nineties, when they'd been married. Beyond that, there were only sporadic images of her, at family gatherings and various functions and Michael had a sudden, awful thought, that by marrying her he'd taken her away from her parents, something this lack of photographic history seemed to prove. But they didn't say anything and seemed grateful that he sat with them into the early hours.

He didn't cry the next day, when he went to the registry office and dealt with all of the paperwork. Or the day after that, meeting with the vicar and undertaker with his father-in-law. Or even when he was asked for Nicola's favourite song, which would play her coffin into church.

Nicola was buried the following Tuesday, in the little churchyard on the hill outside of Gaffney and Michael didn't cry at the graveside.

It took another three days for him to crack. He was making a cup of tea when he realised he couldn't see the kettle properly. In the moment it took to register the tears, they were cascading down his cheeks. He felt a sudden pressure in his chest, took a deep breath and sobbed it out. The tears came heavily then and he slid to the floor, his back to the fridge, sobbing for his wife and everything that had been taken away. He stayed like that for a long time and it never happened again.

Afterwards, he tried, as best he could, to get on with his life. He went back to work, endured conversations with people who told him they knew 'just how he felt' and was amazed he didn't throttle any of them. He let the post build up at home, not wanting to open any more sympathy cards, hating each of them for their perfectly realised pictures of doves and hearts and scrolls, alluding to a state that is serene and peaceful when, in reality, it's anything but.

And he suffered with his insomnia.

But when he did, finally, sleep, he mainly dreamt of the wood and Nicola.

4:

"Please remember, folks, that if you need to have a chat about anything, you can call me at any time."

People got up, wishing their immediate neighbour all the best and went to get their coats. Michael went to wash up his cup and then got his jacket. Saskia was at the doorway, talking to Drew, and Michael watched as he touched her forearm gently. Saskia looked at it, briefly, then bit her lip and wiped away a tear. Drew said something and Saskia nodded, as she pulled her coat on.

"Goodnight," said Michael as he walked by, "thank you for the talk, Drew."

"You're welcome, Michael." He touched Michael's arm to stop him, then pulled out his wallet and took a card from it. "I'm serious about ringing. This has my home and mobile numbers and my email, just in case."

Michael took the card. "Thank you."

"You can get through this, trust me." He looked around, as if to make sure that nobody was standing close. "How long has it been now, about six weeks?"

"Yes."

Drew nodded. "If you have dark thoughts, dark dreams, ignore them."

The words became a blur that Michael couldn't understand. "What does that mean?"

"Exactly what I said." Drew smiled, but it didn't touch his eyes. "Dreams are just what they are, Michael, your mind unwinding at the end of the day."

"You've lost me."

Drew smiled again and this time, his face lit up. "Ah, I'm just being silly. But ring me if you need to."

"I will," Michael said, nodding but confused, "thank you."

Saskia was holding the door to the corridor for him, so Michael rushed over to her. "Thanks."

Slowly, they walked to the exit, Saskia picking at her nails.

"Drew said a weird thing back there," said Michael.

"What about?"

"That I should ignore dark dreams."

Saskia looked as if she was going to laugh, then seemed to check herself. She put her fingertips to her lips and strode for the door.

"What?" Michael called, rushing to catch her up. "Do you know what he means? Is he talking about suicide or something?"

She stopped at the doorway, the yellow wash of the streetlight making her look sick and otherworldly. "I'm not sure, he said the same thing to me, after my first few meetings here. I think he believes that you'll see a place in your dreams, with your loved one guiding you there, but if you follow them, you won't come back."

Michael looked at her, trying to see if this was some kind of weird, sick joke. "Really?"

"Yes."

"What about you, do you believe it?"

"I don't know."

Something about the way she said it struck him. "Have you ever had dreams like that, with your husband?"

"No," she said and Michael knew immediately that she was lying. "People kill themselves for all manner of reasons, not just because they dreamed of a place."

"No, of course not."

"I'll see you in a fortnight," she said, turned and was gone into the darkness, her shoulders hunched against the drizzle, her right hand keeping the neck of her coat together.

Michael watched until she was safely into her car, then ran for his. He sat inside quietly, listening to the hum of rain on the roof, looking out of the soaked windscreen at the distorted world beyond.

Could the dreams that Drew meant be the ones that he'd been having, or was it all some weird coincidence?

Shaking his head, he started the engine and drove back towards the town centre.

Traffic was light and those pedestrians that had braved the weather were either hunched over or sheltering under umbrellas, rushing to get where they needed to go.

Bright lights from fast food outlets splashed primary colours across the pavement and into the gutters, making the street lights seem almost dull. The windscreen wipers, which he'd set on intermittent, struggled with the drizzle as the car picked up speed.

Michael glanced out of the window, saw the traffic lights turning amber at the pedestrian crossing and then it was too late, he was past them and a woman standing at the kerb glared at him.

He slammed on his brakes and the car shuddered to a stop on the wet tarmac. He turned in his seat and called "Sorry", though he knew the woman couldn't hear him. She was glaring at him from the kerb, her clothes soaked, her hair stuck to her head.

He hadn't seen her, his mind elsewhere.

The amber lights flashed and she hurried across the road. He unclipped his seatbelt and opened the door, then stopped. What was he going to do, chase after her to apologise? No, that would just make a bad situation worse.

As he put his seatbelt back on, he thought he saw Nicola. She was across the road, sheltering under the Pizza Plus restaurant awning and the ache of longing and nostalgia was so strong he felt it in his chest. That had been their restaurant and once, on a very rainy night, he'd been held up by traffic and arrived late, to find Nicola standing under the awning, pissed off with him.

He pulled into the kerb and got out. Glancing quickly from left to right for traffic, he ran across the road.

By the time he reached the other side, no-one was standing outside the deserted restaurant that had once been Pizza Plus. The awning was ripped and the chipboard covering the windows was plastered with bills for local bands and various graffiti.

He leaned against the wall, tears mixing with rainwater on his cheeks. He knew that he couldn't have just seen her, however much he wished he had but he missed her so much. The way she talked, the way she laughed and the way she'd say things with a totally straight face that would reduce him to fits of laughter. He missed that it took her so long to get ready, that sometimes her procrastination skills would have shamed a sloth; he even missed the bunched up tissues with lipstick smears that always seemed to find their way onto his chest of drawers. He just wanted her back and wondered if that meant he was still at stage one of Drew's cycle.

5

He was standing on top of the mound, the naked trees making their strange knocking sound.

He looked towards the other copse and saw the woman with red hair again and tried desperately to remember where this place was. He'd been here before, he was sure of it, he and Nicola had…

He started down the mound, slipping and sliding, trying to get a grip to slow himself down but only succeeding in skinning his palms. He stumbled at the base, his ankle shrieking with pain.

"Please, Michael." The voice seemed to come from every direction. "Don't go."

He looked around but he was on his own. "Nic? Where are you?"

"I'm here, like I always said I would be."

Nicola stepped out from behind a tree and tears stung his eyes, his vision swimming. The sun seemed to be shining directly on her, combining with his tears to create a shimmering nimbus around her. Her face was shadowed but he could clearly see her eyes, glimmering with life and vitality.

"Oh, baby…" he said, before his voice cracked and he swallowed back a sob.

She put her finger to his lips and he knew it was there, even though he couldn't feel it. "Ssh, keep quiet, don't wake them."

He wiped the tears from his cheek. "Who?"

"The coughers," she said.

He paused, confused. "What's going on?" he whispered.

"I want you to see that I'm okay, that I'm safe, that you can move on."

"How can you expect me to do that?"

"Mike, you must. The more you dwell on things, the more you'll be drawn back here and I don't want that for you."

"What do you mean? Where am I?"

"Think back, Mike. The wood, the track, the ruins in the trees."

He tried but his mind felt sluggish and unresponsive. Finally, memories began to emerge, of walking with Nicola, cutting through to Compass Wood from…

"Coffers Wood? That's where I am, isn't it? And that place further down is The Mill?"

"Yes."

A sound rang out, like someone hacking their lungs up, echoing around them. Nicola looked towards the source of the noise and seemed frightened.

"What is it?"

"Them," said Nicola, quietly. "Can you not feel it? The ghosts are around us all the time."

"I don't understand."

"Quickly," she said, suddenly standing on his right, startling him. More hacking sounds carried to them. "Get up, you have to move."

"But I don't want to leave you, Nicola."

"Then don't come here again, you must promise me."

"I promise."

When he woke up, long before the alarm which was set to go off at seven, he checked to see if Nicola was lying beside him. Then he checked his palms. To his dismay, they were perfectly fine.

He sat up, silent tears running down his cheeks. Another dream. But at least now he knew where he'd been seeing her.

6.

A dirty brown Cavalier, its exhaust rumbling and harsh dance music blaring through opened windows, came down the road and Michael watched until it disappeared around the corner, the teenaged driver completely oblivious to him, chatting on a mobile phone.

As the noise subsided, Michael turned to look down Mill Lane. This led to the folly, where he'd played as a kid.

Four large bungalows, set back from the lane on sizeable plots of land, looked out over the fields towards Haverton. Beyond them were allotments, two fields the size of football pitches, each featuring a motley array of sheds and dowel tripods for training runner beans.

The lane rose after the allotments. At the crest of this rise was an old farmhouse that Michael remembered being terrified of as a kid — it was out of the way, had a lot of outbuildings that looked cracked and decayed and a huge Alsatian in the yard.

After this, the tarmac stopped and the lane was just hard-packed earth, with occasional slabs and patches of hardcore and a grass strip grew out of the median, like a scruffy Mohican. After the lane turned a corner, Coffers Wood spread out to the left, a "Keep

Out" sign from British Steel posted at a gap in the wooden fence.

The gap was smaller than he remembered, clogged now by adventurous branches from the hedge. He stood as close as he could and peered in, the canopy of branches dappling the leaf-strewn ground, and saw the mound. For the briefest of moments, he felt a sharp chill in his chest and then it was gone. Of course the mound was there; he'd seen it as a kid.

The lane wound on, growing ever more narrow, until it reached the heart of the folly, the remains of Mill House. Or The Mill, as it was known.

He didn't know what it had been — he and his friends came to the conclusion that it might have been a mill — just that it was in ruins when he first discovered it and, talking to his parents, was in ruins for as long as they knew too.

During long, hot summer holidays, Michael and his friends had come here to play war, to cut through to Haverton (through the folly, down the huge field where, if you weren't careful, you'd get chased by the farmer and across the brook on a drainage pipe) or simply to explore. All of those things got less interesting as he hit his teens and he probably hadn't visited the folly for the best part of twenty years.

The lane ended at a small turning area, with fields ahead and to the right, heading down towards the brook. The Mill was to the left, surrounded by trees, occupying perhaps half an acre, two stone gateposts guarding the way, cracked with age now and almost hidden behind years of growth from the hedge.

Michael stood between them and looked around in the gathering dusk. He was alone down here, protected from the noise the main road by the fields and trees, the brook too calm to make a sound that would carry up to him. High in the trees, crows cawed and took flight.

He'd expected to feel something when he stood here, that would help to explain what his dreams meant but he didn't and the realisation choked a small laugh out of him. The sound took something in the hedge to his left by surprise and it darted away noisily.

What was he expecting to find? It was a ruin, a playground, what answers could it possibly contain for his dreams? It was just a place and, sometimes, things are exactly what they appear to be, however desperately you might want their existence to signify something. Looking at it now, as red streaks began to form in the sky above the trees, the more he thought that The Mill just was — it didn't signify or prove anything. It just existed.

He could see that there were still rough paths through the undergrowth, cut down and maintained by generations of Gaffney and Haverton kids playing there, all of which led to the centre and he stepped onto the one in front of him.

It was more overgrown that he remembered and he wondered, for a moment, if kids actually came down here to play anymore. Certainly, someone had, their existence obvious by the bleached fast food cartons, cigarette packets and drink cans that littered the undergrowth bordering the path.

It didn't take long to reach the centre of the site and it was like he'd never been away. The ruined foundations of The Mill dominated the space, the brickwork cut off at ground level. The cellars were still there, three large, rectangular rooms with stone steps leading down into them, the dark-blue brick covered by fading whitewash. A small, shallow ditch ran around the building and, as he had when he was a kid, he thought it looked like a moat. Off to the right, accessible through bracken that snatched at clothes, was a well.

He still didn't feel anything, apart from a warm flash of nostalgia that the place hadn't changed since he was a kid.

"What is it about this place, Nicola?"

Everything was still, even the crows. Michael walked to the edge of the foundations and stepped onto the low ledge, formed from the top of the old wall. It was three-bricks thick here, most of them still as solid as the day they were laid.

He followed the line of the wall, turning left at the first branch, towards Haverton. As he looked over the hedge-line and between the trees towards the brook, he heard a cough. Surprised, he turned around, holding his arms out for balance.

He scanned left and right, squinting into the dusky gloom of the tree line, but couldn't see anyone at all. A faint pulse of unease tugged at him and he knew that it was simply because he was down here, well away from other people and it was getting dark but, really, there was nothing to be worried about. After all, the cougher was either someone coming down the lane the way he had, perhaps walking their dog, or else someone coming up from the brook, maybe taking a shortcut from Haverton to Gaffney.

He turned his attention back to the wall and looked down into the depths of foundations, a drop of perhaps ten foot. The floor was covered by water and he could see himself, peering back. Beyond that, under the surface, there were several piles of dark bricks, obviously from where the building had been brought down. Across from him, along the other wall of this cellar room, a small tree was growing out from a large crack in the whitewashed brick.

Looking down made him feel a bit giddy and unbalanced and he looked up, trying to orient himself. There was a rustling from behind him, as if someone was rushing through the undergrowth towards him and he turned sharply, pebbles of brick and mortar peppering the water. Again, he couldn't see anything except that the bracken on the Haverton side of the foundations was thick, with thorns that were large enough to be seen clearly in the fading light. Nothing could have been rushing through that, it would have been torn to pieces — he must have been mistaken.

Slightly spooked now, he stood still, listening intently. There was the faintest hum of road noise, a few birds calling and a steady drip from somewhere behind him, all things he would expect to hear. Then the rushing noise came again, this time distinctly from his right, from the thick bracken. He glanced over, knowing he wouldn't see anything and the noise stopped as he did so.

From behind and to his left, he heard another cough, followed by more. He turned and caught sight of someone moving quickly behind the first line of trees, their white gown almost luminous in the gloom.

"Who's there?" he shouted, pissed off that someone was obviously trying to scare him. The person didn't slow down or respond, and he kept watch on them, meaning to see where they stopped running. He didn't know yet what he was going to do with them, but at least he'd know where they were.

The person was running between the trees, darting in and out of sight and suddenly Michael realised two things. One was that the gown was too white, almost glowing against the murkiness of the wood and the other was that the runner was moving as if unhindered by the thick undergrowth.

"Hello?" he called. The person didn't slow or acknowledge him, but disappeared behind another tree. Michael watched, waiting for them to reappear and that faint pulse of unease he'd felt before stepped up a gear. He was either being spooked by someone — kids, perhaps, annoyed that their drinking session was being interrupted — or he was going slightly mad, neither of which was something he wanted to prolong any longer than he had to.

Another chorus of coughing broke out behind him and he turned around slowly, trying to maintain his balance. He felt warm now, hot almost and he could accept that he might feel prickly heat with his unease, but it was more than that. It almost felt as though the heat was building and concentrated, like he was standing too close to a bonfire.

Then it was gone, along with the coughing.

Something reflected in the water and caught his eye. He looked down and saw himself and the head of a person who appeared to be standing to his right. It was there and then suddenly gone. The shock of seeing it seemed to fill his head with pins and needles and he fought for a moment to catch his breath. Instinctively, he looked around but he was alone on the wall.

This was too much. "Who's there?" he called, looking along the tree line, hoping to catch a glimpse of the person in white again. "Who is it?"

Bracken snapped behind him and, before he had a chance to turn, he felt hands pressing into the small of his back, pushing him forward. Caught off guard, he felt himself go and windmilled his arms desperately, trying to keep his balance. The hands let go and he knelt down quickly, making himself as small a target as possible. He looked around but he was still alone.

"What do you want?" he called.

Someone coughed, as if in response, a hacking sound from deep within the tree line and it was taken up by more, building into a chorus that seemed to surround him.

Then there was another sound, a word that he could almost but not quite hear, that sounded very much like "Mike". It was gone almost as soon as he heard it but that was it, the final straw. Whatever was happening here, it was intense and potentially dangerous now and he just wanted out of it. Steadily, he got to his feet and walked off the wall as quickly as he could, the coughs fading away as he did so. By the time he reached the hard-packed earth at the edge of the path, the coughing was almost gone, but the feeling of unease was still nagging at him. Without turning back, Michael kept going. The path was darker than before, much darker, the trees and hedges that bordered it cutting out a lot of the light. He could barely see the ground and it made the brisk flight of the person in the gown all the more astounding.

The lane, when he finally reached it, was the most welcome sight he'd seen in weeks and, as he stood on the rough gravel surface, he realised that the coughing had stopped altogether now and that he could hear crows in the trees above him.

7.

"Hello, Drew, it's Michael."

"Hello, how're you?"

"I'm fine, but I need to ask you a question." Michael took a deep breath, suddenly unsure of himself. He'd rehearsed the question all day, until it now seemed like a random collection of words, but he had to ask. "At the last meeting, you said something that's been nagging at me ever since."

"I'm sorry about that, I'd never want to plague your mind with anything."

"I know, it's just that I didn't understand what you meant when you said that if I had dark thoughts, I should ignore them."

"Oh really? You should always ignore dark thoughts, because they often lead to dark deeds and I don't want you to do anything silly."

"Like suicide?"

"Absolutely," said Drew quickly, "that's always a danger. We all have our low moments, but we have to push through them."

"You said something else, about dark dreams. What did that mean?" The line went quiet, until Michael could only hear a faint pulse. "Drew?"

"I'm here."

"Is anything wrong?"

"No, not at all, I'm just thinking."

"About the answer?"

Drew laughed, a humourless chuckle. "We all dream, Michael and some of them push us in certain directions. All I was trying to say was that you shouldn't always follow what you dream."

"But what if the dream feels real?"

"That's just the way it goes, some are vivid, some aren't. I take it you've dreamt of…" There was a slight pause, as Drew tried to recall her name. "…of Nicola?"

"Yes."

"And she seems okay?"

"Yes."

"Excuse my insensitivity but does she look like you remember her, from the end?"

"No, she looks like she did before, when everything was good."

"And have you dreamed of a place?"

Michael felt his pulse quicken. "Yes, I have."

"And where was that?"

"The Mill," said Michael, quietly. There was absolute silence from the other end. "At the bottom of the folly."

"I know where it is," said Drew tersely. "How long have you been having these dreams?"

"Pretty much since Nicola died, but I only recognised it last night."

"Were you told?"

"Yes."

"Okay, Michael, I think we need to talk. Why don't we meet up somewhere?"

"Did you have anywhere in mind?"

"At the library. How would you be fixed for Saturday afternoon?"

8.

Weekends were the worst, Michael had found. At work, if you discounted the ghoulish attention he sometimes received, he was following a routine that had existed before, but Saturday and Sunday were different. He and Nicola had made a point of treating weekends as theirs and for the bulk of the time it was just them — sitting in the garden, watching TV or lying in bed on Sunday and squabbling over who got which supplement.

After she'd gone, he'd been invited to friends' houses and gone willingly, but soon found he didn't want to be there. Conversational topics quickly got strained and he'd lost count of the times somebody had started telling an anecdote, only to realise that Nicola played a part in it before tailing off, embarrassed. Or, worse, talked about how awful something in their life was that made them hate their situation, then looked to Michael for reassurance, as though being told off by your boss compared to losing your wife.

Now, to fill his weekends, he'd taken to walking, spending time at the library or renting films. He tried to avoid crowds because seeing people together, being happy, made him feel sick with nostalgia.

Michael turned into Newland Street just after ten o'clock, which meant he was almost clear of the town centre — just pass the bus-bays, negotiate the

41

crossings at the traffic lights and that was it, back into residential streets.

He passed some shops and then "The Society Of Friends" coffee house. He glanced in as he walked by and saw Saskia, sitting on her own by the window. She was looking out into the street and they seemed to recognise each other at the same time.

She waved and he raised his hand — should he go in and say hello or keep walking? She got up and pointed to the door, which he took to mean she wanted to talk, but did he want to do that? After all, the only thing they had in common was death.

That made him feel guilty, so he slowed to match her pace as she threaded her way between tables.

She pulled open the door and said "Hi" with the overt breeziness of someone trying to cover up their lack of confidence. "This is going to sound really stupid," she gabbled and then paused, patting her chest. "Sorry," she said and let out a small giggle, "I'll understand if you can't, but would you like to have a drink with me? You know, if you're not doing anything, it'd be nice to have a friend to sit with."

Weirdly, the desperation in her voice made him want to agree. "All right," he said.

He followed Saskia to the counter, where she picked up a spare cup and then they wound their way back to her table. She poured him a cup from the stainless steel teapot and slid it to him.

"Thank you."

"You're welcome. So what're you doing in town?"

There was no point in not telling the truth. "Trying to fill my day," he said and watched as she met his eyes briefly, then looked at her cup. "I try to make sure I keep busy at weekends, so that I don't stop and think too much."

She nodded. "I know how that feels."

"Of course," Michael said. "Sorry. Did you want to talk about something else, like the weather?"

She smiled and he thought for a moment that she was actually going to laugh. "No, but definitely something else. Tell me about you."

"Me?" He shrugged. "There's not much to tell, really."

"Everyone has a life story, Michael."

"But I can't tell mine without mentioning Nicola and then I'll get upset and it'll turn into us talking about loss."

"Of course," she said, sipping her tea. "What about a funny story then? Well, not really funny, but different."

"Go on."

"A few years back, long before John was sick, I smoked. He hated it, so I used to do it on the sly, eating whole packets of Polos and thinking he'd never notice." She laughed. "Stupid, eh? I used to smoke whenever I had to go off somewhere on my own and, if there wasn't an opportunity, I'd make one. One Saturday, I went underwear shopping and John hated standing around changing rooms, so I went on my own. I parked in the multi-storey, lit my first fag of the day and it was glorious."

She smiled, wistfully and looked out of the window.

43

"I leaned on the wall and the view was wonderful — the sky was clear as a bell, the sun was high and bright and I could see clear across Gaffney. I was aware of people around me, coming back to their cars and going home and others coming in, you know and then I became aware of someone walking along and I just knew they were coming to me." She looked at Michael. "The person stopped behind me and coughed, so I turned around and it was one of the centre security guards. He smiled and held his hands out, as if he was trying to placate me. 'Are you okay, love?' he said and I didn't know what he was talking about."

"He thought you were going to jump?"

She nodded. "Apparently, there'd been a rash of people throwing themselves off the upper floors so if they saw anyone on CCTV loitering for longer than a minute or so, they'd send someone up to check it out."

"What did you say to him?"

Saskia laughed, lightly. "I told him the truth, that I was having a sneaky fag before I went clothes shopping. He seemed to understand, but he stayed talking to me until I'd finished and then he walked down to the shopping level with me."

"Like he didn't trust you."

She shrugged. "For all he knew, as soon as he'd turned his back on me, I was going to jump. If I was him, I wouldn't have trusted me either."

"That'd be awful, wouldn't it? Knowing that you'd managed to talk someone around and then they kill themselves anyway."

She nodded. "But do you want to know the most ironic thing? Suicide was the furthest thing from my mind that day — I was happy with my life. Why would I want to end something that actually made me wake up with a smile?" She lifted her cup to her chin. "That day I wouldn't and now I find I can't."

Her casually spoken words hit Michael like a slap. "What?"

She didn't look at him. Instead, she watched her fingers play with the handle of her cup. "I've tried to commit suicide." She took a deep breath, let it out slowly. "I'm not proud, that I've attempted it or that I've failed, but that's part of me now, of who I am."

"I didn't realise."

"Why would you?"

"My God, I…" What could he say to her? "When was this?"

"Several times. On the way home from the hospital, just after the funeral, two or three times since then."

"Jesus, Saskia, have you spoken to anyone about this?"

She shook her head and looked at him, her eyes red. "Have you tried?"

That gave him pause — he hadn't. He was devastated by the loss of Nicola, felt that part of his life had been brutally ripped away and missed her like he wouldn't have believed possible, so why hadn't he attempted suicide? Did this make his feelings of grief any less? "No," he said finally, perhaps more to himself than to Saskia. "And if I had, I probably wouldn't have told anyone."

45

"Why?"

"I don't know. Perhaps because then it'd be a cry for help and that's not what it was all about."

Saskia clicked her fingers and pointed at him. "Thank you. I tried because it was what I wanted to do, not for sympathy — if anything, I could have done with less sympathy from people."

"So what happened?"

"Don't ask," she said quietly, and he watched tears fill her eyes.

"I don't know why I haven't tried," he said, after a while, "because being without her hurts so much. Probably the only time it crossed my mind was at the crematorium, as I watched her coffin go behind that curtain, but I didn't do anything."

Saskia pressed her fingers under her eyes. "Do you think I'm weak?"

"Why?"

"Because I tried?"

Without thinking, he reached out and laid his hand over hers but as soon as they touched, he knew he'd made a mistake. They both withdrew their hands quickly and he looked down sheepishly. "Sorry," he said, "I shouldn't have done that."

Saskia looked out of the window and Michael noticed more tears, gathering and glistening on her lower eyelids. The silence that descended on the table seemed heavy and sad, as if breaking it would involve too much effort but leaving it would suffocate them.

"Failing made me feel worse," she said finally, facing him. "He was everything to me and now I don't know what to do." She pressed her fingers under her eyes again. "I miss him, Michael, in more ways than I thought it was possible to miss somebody. You know what I mean, how it feels to be in the house on your own, looking at your past. And the loneliness? My God, the loneliness is the worst thing, that's what pushes me to the limit."

He didn't know what to say, even though he knew what it felt like, the crushing weight of suddenly being alone, however many family and friends you might have around you.

"Everybody suddenly has an opinion on how you feel, based on what they felt when their dog died or something happened to one of their friends, but they never get what I miss the most."

"Which is?"

"Him. The feel and touch of him, his smell, lying next to him in bed and feeling his hands on me. I miss holding him and hugging him and kissing him and making love with him. Is that wrong?"

"Of course not, you're bound to miss all that."

"Do you?"

He supposed he did, but with Nicola in the hospice it had been such a long time since they'd made love that it wasn't foremost of what he missed. "Sort of," he said and explained himself.

"I'm sorry, I didn't realise."

"That's okay."

"This is getting heavy, shall we change the subject?" Saskia said and held her cup up.

He chinked his cup to hers and smiled. "Absolutely."

"When we were at Group, Drew said to you about dark dreams and you asked me if I'd ever seen a place and I said no."

"I remember."

"Well, I lied. I said no because I didn't want to get into a big discussion in case Drew caught up and things kicked off. But I have."

"Did you dream about The Mill?"

She looked at him, as if half of her had expected him to say it and the other half was completely taken by surprise. "Yes, how did you know?"

He told her his dreams.

"Bloody hell," she said. "My dreams started after John died and I don't remember the mound, but I've seen him in the wood and heard the coughing and seen the worried look on his face."

"Have you ever been tempted to go and see what's down there?"

"No," she said, firmly, "I'd be too scared."

Michael looked at her, wanting her to clarify what she meant but she didn't. Instead, she looked out of the window, holding her cup close to her face with both hands, as if her arms were a barricade to keep something away.

They drained the pot of tea in silence.

"I have to go," said Michael and he stood up.

"It's been good to see you," she said and smiled. "Do you have my number? You know, just in case you need to speak to someone who's going through the same thing?"

Whatever had scared her now seemed to have passed and she was gabbling as she had before, self-conscious and shy.

She took a pen from her handbag and scribbled her number on a napkin. He took it and the pen and wrote his number on another napkin. "Thanks," he said, "I appreciate the chat and the tea."

"You're welcome."

9:

Later that afternoon, Drew met Michael in the vestibule of Gaffney library, holding a slim hardback. He shook Michael's hand and led him to the reading room at the back of the library.

Half of the tables were empty, but Drew still made for one at the far end of the room, under a shelf that held two dozen telephone directories. He sat facing the main door and gestured to the seat opposite.

Once Michael had sat down, Drew said, "When did you go?"

"Last night."

"Why?"

"Because I wanted to. I haven't been there since I was a kid and I couldn't work out what the connection was with Nicola, or why I should suddenly start dreaming about it."

"And what happened?"

Not wanting to lead the conversation, Michael said, "Nothing."

Drew rubbed his forehead gently with both hands. "Michael, I'd like to think that we're friends and, even if you don't, you obviously trust me." He knitted his fingers tightly. "If you want me to tell you something, you have to be so kind as to return the favour."

"I don't understand."

"I think you do. Something happened, didn't it, at The Mill?"

Michael bit his lip, trying to think of how to get across what he'd experienced without sounding like an hallucinating fool. "I don't know, I genuinely can't explain what I saw or heard or felt."

The two men stared at one another for a few moments.

"Listen, Michael," Drew said, "I've not come here to make fun of you, okay?" He worried his lower lip, pulling at it with his fingers. "I've never told anybody this, but it might help. When Simon died, I didn't know what to do with myself. Everything around me reminded me of him, so I took to walking, out of Gaffney and into the countryside, head down and focusing on the road, just trying to get my feelings out and cry when there was nobody around to ask me how I felt. Well, one day I decided to go to Haverton and cut down through the folly."

Drew leaned back in his chair. "I hadn't been there for years, since I was a kid probably and I was amazed that it was exactly how I remembered it, and then I saw The Mill itself. Something was nagging at me, goodness knows what because the place was in ruins when I was a kid and I wasn't scared of it, as such, but I didn't want to go through there. So I decided to cut through the field behind The Mill and then along to the main road. My days of climbing over drainage pipes are long gone, I'm afraid."

Both men smiled at one another.

"As I was walking past the entrance, I heard a cough. I assumed it was someone coming up from the brook and kept going, keeping an eye out for them. I'm quite jumpy, so I wanted to be ready for them, otherwise I'd have scared us both, leaping around like an idiot. But nobody came out and then I heard Simon."

"Really?"

Drew smiled, as if he'd run through this story in his mind a hundred times, knowing that people would smirk and think he was losing his marbles. "As real as I'm sitting in front of you. 'D babe', he said, 'come and see me, I'm lonely'. Nobody would know that he called me D babe, that was just between me and him."

"So what did you do?"

"What do you think, Michael? I'd been to my husband's funeral the week before, I saw him at the funeral home before that, I knew he'd gone. There was no way he could have been in The Mill, calling me. I refused to believe it and kept walking. Sometimes, now, I wish I'd gone in, just to see what might have happened, but I walked into the field and kept going until I couldn't hear him any more." Drew rubbed his eyes. "I believed in ghosts until Simon passed away and then I stopped. After all, if he could haunt me, surely he'd have done it at home and told me how he was and that I'd be okay without him, that he would wait for me to join him. But having said that, I do believe in other things that can draw you into a situation you don't want to be in."

"Such as?"

"There's something weird in The Mill, Michael and I don't understand what it is. Most people I've spoken to, who grew up in Gaffney, played there as kids and never had any problems with the place, unless they got ambushed by Haverton kids. But when someone's bereaved — and this doesn't happen with everyone — and they're looking for something, however unconsciously, that's the place they always seem drawn to."

"Fucking hell."

"So you saw something?"

"Sort of." Michael told Drew what had happened and, when he was done, they looked at one another without speaking. "So," Michael said finally, "what do you think it is?"

Drew tapped his fingers against the book on the table in front of him. "I don't know. Most people are too embarrassed to admit they've seen or heard anything and, after a while, they write it off in their own minds as some kind of hallucination. If they can, of course."

"What does that mean?"

"Okay, Michael, let's get this straight. The other night I said to you that I wanted you to be careful and to not follow your dreams. When you rang me, I said to you about not doing anything silly and you mentioned suicide."

"I remember."

"I didn't mean that I thought you were contemplating suicide, it's just that The Mill has a bit of a history for it."

"Really?"

"Yes, but any location that's far from the madding crowd can be a suicide blackspot. If somebody wants to end it all and it's not a cry for help, they need to be away from do-gooders who'll try and save them. The thing is, The Mill's had more than its fair share over the years and, if you cross-reference enough local history books, it seems to come in cycles."

Michael looked at Drew's earnest expression and shook his head — things were piling up quicker than he could get to grips with them.

"Maybe I'm just a silly man who's read too much and put two and two together and got forty-five. After I heard Simon, I decided to find out what the hell The Mill was, because I'd called it that since I was a kid and never known why. And neither did my mum, when I asked her. But we've had a few characters in this town over the years, some of whom have wanted to immortalise their lives and their weird little ways and they've kept a history for us."

Drew opened the book and lifted it up, to show Michael a photograph plate on the right-hand page. Black and white, it showed a large, three-storey mansion with trees behind it and a large drive sweeping past the front. An ornate fountain was at the bottom of some steps leading from the front door. Three people were standing in front of the fountain, a man and two women, none of them close enough to be able to discern their features clearly.

"This picture was taken in 1869," said Drew. "The man is Richard Manley-Vale, who was a very prominent local businessman. The woman next to him is his wife, Anna and the other woman is his sister, Elizabeth."

Drew put the book on the table and read aloud, keeping his voice low. "'The Mill, once owned by the Manley-Vale family, is situated at the bottom of the Folly in Gaffney. Surrounded by trees, it was once a very grand residence though only the foundations and cellars remain today. In the late 19th century, the last of the Manley-Vale line — Elizabeth, a spinster — decided to give her 'wonderful home' back to the community and it was converted into a hospice for the palliative care of TB sufferers. Unfortunately, some good folk of Gaffney believed in vampirism and never took kindly to the hospice or its residents and so they torched it. Most of the sufferers were burned alive and those that weren't didn't last long either. It was terrible, by all accounts. Since then, the area has fallen into disarray and no other buildings have been constructed there.'"

"I never knew that."

"Neither did I. It's not exactly hidden, since it's in this book, but it doesn't tend to get spoken of very often and it's certainly not part of any oral history of Gaffney, so far as I can tell."

"But what does this have to do with your husband, or what I saw?"

"I don't know, Michael, but I do know that a lot of people who've lost loved ones and been drawn to The Mill have experienced things they couldn't explain. Sadly, a few have taken their lives there." He closed the book gently. "I sound like a madman, don't I?"

Before, Michael would have agreed immediately but things weren't quite so black and white now. He'd experienced things — dreaming about Nicola and seeing her in the rain, everything about The Mill — that his rational mind couldn't explain. Perhaps that was it, the very fact that he couldn't explain what was happening in his life allowed him to accept things that couldn't be explained themselves.

"Maybe, maybe not," he said finally.

Drew smiled. "My point is, something terrible happened at The Mill, a lot of people lost their lives and I find it odd that it seems to have a draw on the recently bereaved. But if you're not there, you can't do anything silly there, can you?"

"Do you still dream about it?"

"Yes, I do. Just be careful, Michael. Your mind is not your best ally at the moment."

"Maybe not. But thank you, for telling me all this."

"Sometimes, the best we can do is pass on what we know," said Drew. "Plus, I like you, I want to see you at more meetings and see you getting stronger each time."

They chatted idly for a while, until Drew looked at his watch and declared that he had to be going. They shook hands at the library doors and Michael watched him walk away, towards the Corn Market car park.

10:

Once Drew was out of sight, Michael walked down the slight hill to Market Street. His phone rang.

"Hello?"

"Michael, is that you?" He didn't recognise the voice, which sounded thick and distant.

"Yes, who's this?"

""It's Saskia. I need to talk to you, in person."

"Okay, when?"

"Now'd be brilliant. Can you come to mine?"

"I don't know where you live."

"Armada Street, number seven, on the estate by the hospital."

"I could be there in half an hour, I'm in town at the moment."

"That's fine," she said, "goodbye".

The line went dead before Michael could respond.

As soon as Michael saw Saskia, when she opened the door, he got a bad feeling about having turned up. Her eyes were red, slightly glazed and it felt as if she were looking through him, rather than at him — that's why she'd sounded so distant on the phone, she wasn't quite on the planet anymore.

"Are you okay?"

She smiled, lazily. "Yes, come in."

She stepped back, holding tightly to the door and he passed her. Once he was in the hall, she closed the door gently and deliberately, as if pretending not to be intoxicated.

"Did you want to come through to the kitchen? I was just getting a late lunch and I can make you a sandwich, if you want."

"That'd be nice," he said.

She led him down the hall to her large, well-appointed kitchen. She walked over to a worktop, her bare feet slapping on the tiled floor and stood in front of a chopping board, her back to him. He looked at her, dressed in expensive jeans and a plain khaki T-shirt and felt sorry for her — drunk before the evening, making a snack for someone she barely knew but desperately wanted to speak to.

"We're having cold chicken," she said.

"Lovely," he said and leaned against a worktop, folding his arms. "So, do you live alone?"

She nodded. "Afraid so. We'd always planned to have kids but I kept putting it off because we both had good jobs and enjoyed our foreign holidays. I thought we could start when I hit my mid-thirties, perhaps have a couple and enjoy being homebodies for a while."

"That's nice." She turned her head slightly, then went back to making the sandwich. "I'm sorry," he said quickly, "that was insensitive."

"No, it's not that, it's just… You're right, it was a nice idea, a good plan, until John went and ruined it."

He didn't want to talk about death again, so he changed the subject. "You said you wanted to talk?"

The knife blade clanged heavily, twice, against the glass chopping board. "I did." She reached into a cupboard level with her head and took out two plates.

"About anything in particular?" he prompted.

"Not really." She turned and handed him a plate with a thick sandwich on it, some of the chicken falling away from the bread, then leaned on the worktop, holding her plate against her belly, her T-shirt pulled tight over her breasts. He looked away, ill at ease.

"I just thought that, as we've both been widowed, it'd be nice to see you and have a chat and some food."

He felt awful, her words seeming to hang in the air, taunting him. He'd automatically thought it was a bad idea, turning up, because she was drunk and then, to top it off, he'd stared at her breasts. What kind of pervert was he?

She smiled at him. "You're not very impressed that I've had a little drinky, are you?"

"Saskia, it's none of my business."

"During the week, I'm as straight as a die and at the weekend, I have a drink. I mean, there's only me — who cares if I couldn't drive a car now or if I fall asleep watching TV? No-one does." She looked out of the window, tapping her fingers against her lips. "I saw how you looked at me when I opened the door and, to tell you the truth, I'd probably have felt the same way except that now, I know exactly why I'm drinking."

"It's okay, really."

"Did you want a drink?"

"No, but thank you."

She took a half-empty bottle of white wine out of a cupboard and filled a glass that was on the worktop. "Cheers," she said and took a gulp. "So, what were you doing when I rang, it sounded noisy."

"I was in town." Although he wasn't sure it was a good idea, he said, "I saw Drew and we talked about The Mill. He says there's something there — he's dreamt about the place and heard his partner calling his name from there."

Saskia put her wineglass down, her mouth dropping open slightly. "No."

"I've been there too."

"What?"

Michael told her what had happened to him and the bare bones of his conversation with Drew.

"Do you believe what you saw was real?" she asked.

"Yes."

"Did you feel better, about everything, afterwards?"

"No, it scared the shit out of me. Talking with Nicola in the dream was nice, but she wasn't in The Mill."

"What do you suppose it is?"

He shrugged. "I don't know."

"What if it's the place? I've read stuff like this, what if the pain and suffering of those poor people was imprinted onto The Mill?" Animated now, she didn't wait for an answer. "If something's lingering there, maybe that's why we're dreaming of our loved ones. Perhaps we somehow tap into a primal state, where these things can see us and communicate with us?"

"Saskia, if that was the case, surely everyone would know about it?"

"What if they do?" she asked, excitement almost tangible in her voice, "but they're too scared to say?"

"What do you mean?"

Her eyes were bright, as if the conversation was sobering her up rapidly. "If someone told you there was a place where you could access spirits from generations ago, you'd think they were a nutter. But if you're bereaved, talking to others who've suffered a loss, it's different — we won't dismiss it out of hand because we want to believe it. Who wouldn't want to contact their loved one?"

He suddenly realised that he'd said too much, had got her hopes up. "Saskia, what I saw and felt wasn't Nicola. It scared me, I won't be going back there and I don't think you should go, either."

"Why not?" she asked, setting her shoulders like a petulant child.

"Because something's wrong with the place — I felt uncomfortable and Drew won't go anywhere near it." He looked at her, imploring her with his eyes. "Promise me?"

She lifted her wine glass and drained the contents. "Okay," she said, putting the glass firmly on the worktop.

"Good. When we next meet up, we can ask Drew more questions, all right?"

"Fine," she said, dragging the word out like it was painful to say.

"You sound like it's not."

She looked at him, dipping her head slightly. "You could say that."

"See, I can read you like a book."

She laughed, longer and harder than the comment deserved, as if she needed to release tension. He didn't believe for an instant that she'd paid much attention to his warning and wished he'd kept his mouth shut.

She poured herself another glass full of wine. "So what else shall we talk about?"

He took a bite of his sandwich. "What are your plans for the rest of the weekend?"

She walked across the kitchen to stand next to him and put her plate on the worktop. She rubbed her hand on her T-shirt and he looked away quickly, but not before he saw her breast move freely under the thin material. Why was he looking at her like this?

"No plans. Like I said to you before, there's not a lot in my life now. I go to work, come home and eat, watch TV and have a drink, then I go to bed and it all starts again the next day."

"I'm sorry, I…"

"Why do you keep apologising? It's not your fault that I'm lonely. I'm not proud of it but it's nothing to be ashamed of either, it's just the way things are. I mean, aren't you lonely?"

"Sometimes."

She touched his arm and he jumped slightly. Her fingers were cool and smooth. "You miss her, don't you?"

"Yes," he said, "very much."

"We both miss our lovers."

"Yes," he said, getting more uncomfortable all the time. He knew it was the drink talking but, even so, he knew that he was going to have to leave.

"That's why it's so important to have good friends, who understand what we're going through."

She rested against him, her head on his chest, still stroking his arm. He tried to tell himself it was just a hug but he knew it wasn't and couldn't bring himself to hold her.

"We're in the same place, Michael, we need the same thing."

He looked into her eyes. "But, Saskia…"

"Kiss me, Michael."

"I can't."

"Kiss me, please."

"No, Saskia," he said, as gently as he could. "If I do, we'll both regret it as soon as it happens."

"I won't, I promise." She sounded agitated now. "Why won't you kiss me?"

He held her arms, as gently as he could whilst letting her know that he was serious and moved her back slightly. "Don't do this. I'll go and we'll forget all about it, okay?"

He let go of her and she stood where he'd put her, her arms by her sides, her head down. "Don't you find me attractive?"

"Yes, you're very attractive, but it'd be wrong."

"How do you know?"

"I don't, but I'm pretty sure. Look, I'll speak to you soon."

He sidestepped around her and walked quickly along the hallway.

"Don't go," Saskia called as he unlatched the door, "please…"

"There's no problem," he called back, "don't worry."

"Please, Michael," she said, tears evident in her voice, "don't go."

He closed his eyes, not wanting to leave her upset but fearing that if he stayed, things would get a lot worse.

He closed the door behind him and walked away, convinced that he could still hear her crying.

11:

Michael walked out of the estate. A large lorry was wheezing its way up Hospital Hill, trailing a line of traffic, so he stood at the kerb, waiting for a gap so that he could cross.

He tilted his head back and rocked it from side to side, his neck creaking slightly and then looked across the road. Nicola was standing in the shade of a tree, looking at him.

Startled, he stepped off the kerb but a blaring horn forced him back. He waved away the driver's angry hand signals and looked at his wife.

She smiled at him and nodded.

He smiled back, as a shuttle bus went by. He caught glimpses of Nicola through the dirty, tinted windows but when the bus had gone past, she wasn't there any more.

But he knew he'd seen her, that he hadn't just thought it.

Or had he?

Like he'd thought that Saskia was coming onto him. What if that wasn't the case, that she just wanted someone to give her comfort? He couldn't do it, because it would feel like a betrayal of Nicola but also, it would be a betrayal of Saskia too — that had been the wine talking back there and, if he'd done as she wanted, how would that have made either of them feel? How could he sit next to her again and pretend like nothing had happened.

With that thought, a weight seemed to hit him. If he'd been embarrassed by this, how must she be feeling now, having pleaded with him as he rushed to escape? What must be going through her mind? Would she now lock herself away, not wanting to go to the group because of him, spending her days working and going home to an empty house, staring at the same four walls every night before succumbing to some kind of stir crazy madness as the loneliness of her situation dug ever deeper into her mind.

He turned around, rubbing his face. He had to go back and tell her everything was okay, that he'd over-reacted and shouldn't have left like he did.

Michael rapped the knocker, hard, then peered through the lounge window. The room was empty.

"Shit."

Michael knocked with his knuckles, as hard as he could but there was still no response. Maybe she'd seen him walking up the drive, couldn't face him and so was hiding. He rapped again, then knelt down and pushed the letterbox open slightly.

"Saskia? It's Michael. I need to speak to you, about before."

Gravel crunched behind him and he whirled around, expecting to see Saskia but it was a man in his late fifties, with a shock of white hair and a ruddy face.

"Can I help you?"

"I'm looking for Saskia."

"I can see that."

"I was just here."

"I saw you."

"I need to speak to her. Do you know if she's gone out?"

"She left, a few minutes after you did. She looked very upset and I was saying to my wife that maybe we ought to ask her if everything was all right, after all that's happened?"

"Which way did she go?"

"Do I strike you as being the kind of neighbour who stands at the window and watches to see where people go."

"No," said Michael, "of course not. It's just important that I speak to Saskia."

"She looked very upset."

"I think she was."

"Did you do that to her?"

"No," Michael lied, not wanting to get into that discussion, "but I want to try and help make things better."

"Because, you know, if you did upset her…"

"I have to go," said Michael and he strode down the driveway. It wasn't until he reached the pavement that he guessed where he was going to go. Saskia was sad, lonely, upset — there was only one place she would go. He just had to hope he got to The Mill before she did.

By the time he reached the mouth of Mill Lane, the daylight had faded enough that the farmhouse at the crest of the hill was shrouded in a haze of twilight.

It was getting cooler now, the air becoming crisp and he leaned on a wall to get his breath back from jogging, his throat and lungs burning. He hadn't seen Saskia on the way here and pushed on, ignoring the stitch in his side, trying to keep up the same pace on the uneven surface after the farmhouse.

The sound of coughing drifted to him through the trees of Coffers Wood. It was some distance away but seemed to be getting closer. He tried to shut the sound out and keep moving.

"Michael." He knew a voice wasn't really calling his name, that it was just the breeze catching the trees and rustling the dying, brittle leaves on them, but it still chilled him. "Michael, don't go…"

Twigs snapped, out of his line of sight and it sounded as if someone was coming for him behind the hedge. He pushed himself harder, running now, keeping his eyes on the uneven and treacherous path.

He slowed at the bend. The field behind the fence had been stripped bare of whatever it had once nurtured, the earth dark. Lights from the road beyond were visible in snatches, showing through where the ruts in the field were deep enough.

Saskia was still nowhere in sight. He pushed himself harder as the path sloped down. His foot caught the edge of a rut, turning his ankle and he fell over, winding himself. Lying on his back, gasping for breath, his ankle singing with pain, he stared at the tops of the trees that lined the lane and the faint wisps of clouds in the gathering darkness of the sky.

"Fuck," he hissed, his breath coming in short, sharp bursts. Gingerly, he investigated his ankle with his fingertips and, whilst it hurt, it wasn't so painful that he would pass out. He rolled over and got up slowly, holding onto a tree trunk for support.

As his breathing settled he could hear more coughing, carried on the wind whispers and looked up the lane, expecting to see people walking towards him. But no-one was there, he appeared to be all alone.

"Saskia?" he yelled, "are you here?"

There was no response. Was she down here or had he made a massive error of judgement? He didn't know but couldn't turn back now. He tested his leg carefully and it didn't buckle, so he hobbled on as quickly as he could. The lane, bordered by high hedges, was dark and visibility was low. The Mill itself seemed to glow, through the haze of dusk, an almost flickering light that picked at the trees, sending shafts of light out into the darkness around it.

"Saskia!"

The only response was from behind him, sounds of feet on gravel and of legs pushing through crops that weren't there. There was more coughing too, some of it deep and sharp, some of it higher-pitched. He knew it was all in his head, that it couldn't be what he thought it was, but he didn't dare turn around, didn't want to see what was coming, just in case he was wrong.

The gateposts appeared out of the murk and he cut across towards them, hoping he didn't stumble into another pot-hole, his ankle still throbbing. As he left the gravel, it suddenly seemed to get darker — too dark, almost pitch — and then he was in the grounds of The Mill and it was light. There was no discernible source for it, but there seemed to be a glow in the air, as bright as a child's nightlight. To his left, looking back towards Coffers Wood and Gaffney, all was dark. To the right, the lights of Haverton twinkled in the night.

"Saskia," he called, ploughing along the rough path, ignoring the pain in his lungs and ankle. "I know you're here, talk to me!"

As if in response, there was an explosion of white and orange light from the centre of The Mill. Almost blinded, he stopped and rubbed his eyes, white stars dancing across his eyelids. When he opened his eyes again, he could see more — as if the intensity of the night-light had been turned up.

The sounds of people coming towards him, down the lane and across the fields, were getting louder so he pushed on, towards the centre of The Mill.

Something crashed through the bush to his left, breathing heavily and he instinctively jerked to his right, twisting his ankle again and falling against a blackened tree stump. As he clamoured for purchase on the splintered bark, he heard more ragged breath from behind him. To his right, to his left, in front — he seemed to be surrounded by the sound.

He dragged himself forward and rolled into the shallow ditch, the chill from the ribbon of water in the base of it making him gasp. He propped himself up to peer over the edge and was so shocked it took him a moment or two to realise what he was looking at.

There were at least a hundred translucent people in front of him, milling around the foundations, heads down. All of them were wearing formless white gowns, their legs and feet bare.

Through the knot of legs, Michael could see Saskia. She stood out vividly, her red jacket bright against the almost glowing whiteness of the people around her and the dark brick of the foundations.

She was on her belly, her head over the ledge, her feet making a V-shape, her toes together.

"Saskia?" The milling crowd either didn't see him or chose to ignore him. "Saskia?"

She rolled to her right slightly and when he saw her face, he almost didn't recognise her. He'd never known her before John died, had never seen what she looked like when the death of a loved one wasn't draped over her like a distorting cloak, but knew she must have looked like she did now. Her eyes were bright, her cheeks had blossoms of colour, her lips seemed redder and fuller and she was smiling.

"Michael," she said, her voice faint as if she was a lot further away from him than she looked. "It's so beautiful, I wish I'd known about this before."

"About what?"

"Michael, it's wonderful. John is here, my dad is here, they're all around, can't you see them?"

He glanced around, searching for some familiar faces, but there was nobody in the shambling mass that he recognised.

"It's so good to see him," Saskia said, grinning brightly, "he wants me to join him."

Michael felt something cold surge through his chest. "No, Saskia, stay there."

She frowned briefly, then it was gone. "Why?" she asked, cheerfully.

He didn't know for sure what he meant, just that this was all wrong and he crawled out of the ditch. Some of the shamblers looked down at him now and he could see their faces clearly, their skin tight, eyes dull and lips drawn. He could hear more laboured breathing and coughing now, but nothing else, not even the hum of traffic.

Saskia leaned back over the ledge. "Yes," he heard her say, "of course I will."

The cold feeling in his chest worked its way up, catching his breath in his throat. His hands sank into soft grass and soil, the feet of the shambling mass appearing to tread on him, though he couldn't feel them.

Saskia knelt up, her back to him and slowly got to her feet. She held out her arms, as if ready for an embrace and he saw her eyelids flicker and close.

Deep down, he knew what she was going to do and realised he wouldn't reach her in time. "Saskia, please don't," he called.

She paid him no heed and stepped forward, her left foot seeming to hang in space just beyond the bricks. Her arms reached out and around, as if she thought that someone was standing in front of her and then she leaned forward.

She dropped out of sight quickly and he heard a heavy splash. As quickly as he could, he made his way to the edge of the foundations and lay flat, half on the bricks, half on the grass, looking down.

Saskia was lying on her side, her head twisted awkwardly, her left arm obviously broken and folded beneath her. She was still smiling, even as blood swirled in the shallow water around her head.

He closed his eyes, tears burning them.

"Michael? What's wrong?"

He knew Nicola couldn't be here, knew it in the same way the shambling people couldn't be wandering around the foundations of The Mill, where so many of them had perished in the fire. He knew it with a total and complete conviction and yet he opened his eyes because he wanted to see her.

The Mill was as bright as day now and Nicola was the only person he could see. He wasn't lying on the edge of a foundation any more, but on a concrete floor. Nicola was standing two or three yards in front of him, wearing her favourite blue dress, her feet bare.

She looked wonderful. Her hair was black and glossy, shining in the light and her skin looked tanned and youthful. Her eyes were so green they almost seemed to glow and her lips were so red he just wanted to kiss her immediately.

"Michael, thank goodness."

"Nicola," he said, "I don't understand."

She raised her arms. "Hold me, please."

"I've missed you," he said.

Tears ran down her cheeks, glistening against her skin. "I've missed you so much it's been painful."

He stood up, favouring his ankle.

"Give me a cuddle," she said and took a step towards him.

He reached out, wanting to touch her and know she was here, to feel her body against him again. His hand touched her skin and he felt the warmth and then it was through, but that didn't matter.

"I love you, Michael," she said.

Michael reached out to embrace her, felt a brief burst of warmth and then nothing.

"I love you too," he said and then he was falling

ABOUT THE AUTHOR

 Mark West was born in 1969 and lives in Northampton-shire, England with his wife, Alison and their young son Matthew. Writing since the age of eight, he discovered the small press in 1998 and since then has had almost sixty short stories published in various magazines around the world. His first collection, *Strange Tales*, was published by Rainfall Books in 2003 and they also published his short novel, *Conjure*, in 2009. His debut novel, *In The Rain With The Dead*, appeared from Pendragon Press in 2005 and following this — and the birth of his son — he spent two years wrestling with writer's block. This was broken when his story *The Mill*, which Mark Morris called 'one of the most moving pieces of writing I have read in a long time', appeared in the acclaimed five-author collection *We Fade To Grey*, edited by Gary McMahon.

Forthcoming publications include the eBook edition of *The Mill*, also through Greyhart Press, plus two novellas and a handful of short stories. West is currently working on a novel and can be contacted

through his website at www.markwest.org.uk or on
Twitter @MarkEWest

ABOUT GREYHART PRESS

Talk to us on Twitter (@GreyhartPress) or email (editors@greyhartpress.com)

www.greyhartpress.com

Greyhart Press is an indie publisher of quality genre fiction: fantasy, science fiction, horror, and some stories that defy description.

We publish eBooks through online retailers. That's great for us and for you, because we don't have to worry about all that costly hassle of printing and distribution. Instead we can concentrate on finding great stories AND giving some away for free! Visit our free story promotion page for no-strings-attached free downloads.

But we love print too, so we're bringing selected stories to paperback starting spring 2012.

Our motto is *Real Stories for Real People!* What's that about, then? It's about the Real Story Manifesto (credit where it's due: this is inspired by the Agile Software Development Manifesto).

We seek to tell great stories by writing them and helping others to find them.
Through this (highly enjoyable work) we have come to value:

Writing clarity over writing style.
Plots that move over plots that are clever.
Characters who make hard choices over characters who observe interesting events.
A reader left satisfied over a critic left impressed.

That is, while there is value in the items on the right, we value the items on the left more.

DO YOU WANT FREE EBOOKS?

If so, our READ... REVIEW... REPEAT... promotion is for you. Follow @GreyhartPress or see our website for more details, even if you aren't on Twitter. You could qualify to read all our eBooks for free!

OTHER TITLES YOU MIGHT ENJOY

Since our beginning in spring 2011, Greyhart Press has added new authors and new titles to our range of eBooks: short stories, novellas, novelettes, novels, and even sagas in verse. During spring 2012 we will add paperback titles too. Here are a couple of picks that readers of *The Mill* might enjoy:

In the Rain with the Dead (an edgy horror novel by Mark West) eBook list price $2.99 / £2.06.

Ten years after the incident with the Ouija board, Nadia and Jim meet at a friend's funeral and fall in love again. This time their love will be real and lasting. But their friend had raised from the dead a disciple of Satan named Megellan. When he smells the purity of Jim and Nadia's affection, his master orders him to rend and corrupt their love. Magellan obeys with relish.

In the Rain with the Dead is both a horror novel and a romance set in the tired English town of Gaffney. But be warned, this is not a vampire-lite paranormal romance. Satan's undead disciple is pure evil; there are a few very strong scenes indeed!

Terminus (a space opera/ horror novel by Paul Melhuish)

Sii Terminus is a space-gannta, a loser crewing deep-space freighters whose best friend is a bottle of snakki. Until one day he is chosen to command an unusual mission to ferry a diplomat to the obscure, dead world of Thanatos One. Except the planet is not as dead as it seems, and Terminus has not been chosen by accident...

Hammer Horror meets *Aliens* in this fast-paced tale of horror, love, and betrayal, where the fate of all humanity rests on the actions of an anti-hero with a hangover.

If you liked *Babel,* you will **love** this!

~Special offer~ Terminus is available during spring 2012 for the introductory eBook list price of 99c /77p. A paperback edition will come later in 2012.

Printed in Great Britain
by Amazon